Skater Boy

Maria Cleary

Illustrated by Lorenzo Sabbatini

Play Station 1

1 Match.

A helmet
B skateboard
C wrist guards
D knee pads
E skate shoes
F elbow pads

2 Read and match.

A You wear these to protect your hands and wrists.
B You use this to move and do tricks.
C You wear this to protect your head.
D You wear these on your feet.
E You wear these to protect your legs and knees.
F You wear these to protect your arms and elbows.

- elbow pads
- skateboard
- wrist guards
- helmet
- knee pads
- skate shoes

3 Read, listen and write.

- bench
- tree
- swing
- slide
- gate
- mothers
- climbing frame
- birds

4 Write.

In the park in my town there is .... and ....

....

....

....

Play Station 1

5 Read and match.

A

B

C

D

- ( ) She is playing chase and she is running.
- ( ) They are sitting on the bench and they are talking.
- ( ) He is playing 'Skater Boy' and he is laughing.
- ( ) He is playing hide and seek and he is hiding behind a tree.

2

6 Listen and tick (✔).

( )

( )

7 Listen. Say the chant. Then read, match and mime.

CHANT

A What are you doing?
I'm hopping. I'm hopping.
It's called hopscotch!

B What are you doing?
I'm skipping. I'm skipping.
Why don't you watch?

C What are you doing?
I'm running. I'm running.
Want to play chase?

D What are you doing?
I'm skating. I'm skating.
Let's have a race.

8 Mime. Ask and answer with a friend.

What are you doing?

I'm skipping.

4 "What's that?" ask the people in the street as they turn their heads to look.
"Look out!" shout the mothers to their children as they hold their hands.
It's Skater Boy. He's the fastest child in town.

Turn your head to look.
Who is:
• behind you?
• on your right?
• on your left?
SWOOSH!

But Skater Boy is too fast.
They can't see him.

When the mothers turn around,
he's not there.
And when the children wave at him,
he's not there.
Where is Skater Boy?

In the park the children play
ball and skipping and chase and
hopscotch and hide and seek.

But their favourite game
of all is: Skater Boy!

And at night when the children go to bed, they dream about Skater Boy, too.

What can you see? Look and point.

- a light
- a clock
- a book
- a bed
- a cap
- Skater Boy

But the mothers aren't happy.
They don't like Skater Boy.
"Who's that boy?
Where does he come from?
What's his name?" they ask.

One day, the mothers are talking in the park.
And the children are playing Skater Boy.
The mothers have a plan.

They want to stop Skater Boy. They don't want their children to play Skater Boy or dream about Skater Boy any more.

Look at the children in the picture.

Ask a friend.
I've got yellow shoes. Who am I?

They are talking and talking. And they don't see Baby.
Baby is climbing and climbing and climbing.
Now he's at the top of the climbing frame.
Oh no! Baby looks down. He's scared.
"Help!" Baby shouts at the top of his voice.

What do you climb with?
Tick (✔).

☐ your hands and feet
☐ your head and nose
☐ your eyes and hair

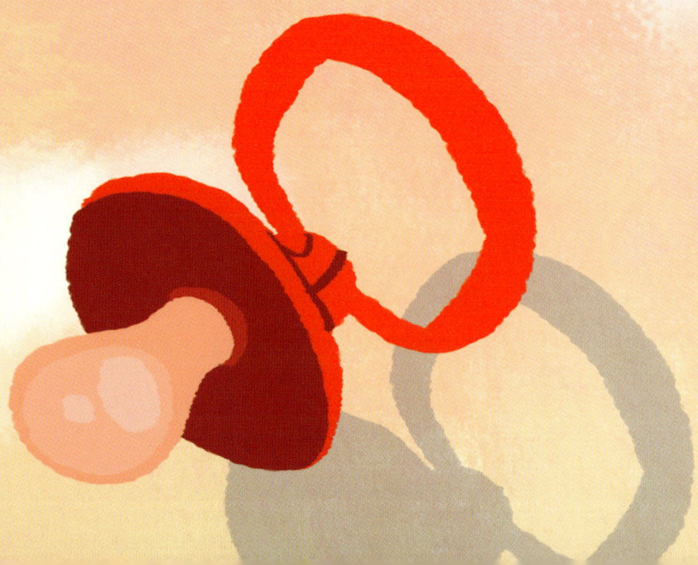

The mothers look up. They see Baby and they run to the climbing frame.
“Mummy!” shouts Baby.
“Don’t move!” shout the mothers.
But Baby starts to fall.

Guess.
Can the mothers
save Baby?

Swoosh!
Find a rubber.
Throw it up into the air.
Can you catch it?
Can you now hand it to a friend?

“What’s that?” say the mothers.
“Look out!” shouts Skater Boy as he races under the climbing frame.
He catches Baby just before he falls.
“Just in time,” says Skater Boy and he hands Baby to his mother.

The mothers are happy and surprised.
They don't know what to say.
"Thanks," says Baby's mother.
Skater Boy smiles. He turns to the children.
"Who wants to play with me?" he asks.
"Me! Me! Me!" shout all the children.
And all the mothers smile. They now know:
the children are safe with Skater Boy.

Ask and answer with your friends.

Who wants to play with me?

Play Station 2

1 Look, read and match.

A

B

C

D

- (B) The children play 'Skater Boy' in the park.
- (A) Baby falls from the climbing frame.
- (C) The mothers talk about Skater Boy.
- (D) Skater Boy saves Baby.

2 Talk to a friend. Say what they are doing in the pictures.

A Baby is falling from the climbing frame

B The children are playing "Skater Boy" in the par

C The mothers are talk about Skater Boy.

D Skater Boy is saving the Baby

3 **Complete the sentences with the correct verbs.**

are
play
want
falls
like
is
climbs
catches

A Skater Boy .... the fastest child in town.

B The children .... Skater Boy.

C The mothers don't .... Skater Boy.

D Baby .... the climbing frame.

E Baby .... from the climbing frame.

F Skater Boy .... Baby.

G The children .... to play with Skater Boy.

H The children .... safe with Skater Boy.

4 **Find 18 words from the story (→↓).**

H	B	R	N	S	A	F	E	X	S
E	F	A	L	L	R	P	A	R	K
L	J	C	A	T	C	H	S	U	A
P	A	E	P	L	A	Y	T	N	T
L	G	S	H	O	U	T	R	G	E
S	U	R	P	R	I	S	E	D	R
M	O	T	H	E	R	S	E	C	B
D	R	E	A	M	B	Z	T	E	O
H	O	P	S	C	O	T	C	H	Y
C	L	I	M	B	G	A	M	E	U

Play Station 2

5 **Read, listen, match and point.**

A

B

C

D

- ◯ fastest
- ◯ youngest
- ◯ smallest
- ◯ tallest

6 **Read and write true sentences.**

A The tallest child in my class is ....

B The youngest child in my class is ....

D The fastest child in my class is ....

E The smallest thing on my desk is a ....

7 Look and write about Skater Boy's family.

- thinnest
- oldest
- prettiest
- youngest
- tallest
- fattest

A Sister is the .... person in the family.

B Grandpa is the .... person in the family.

C Mum is the .... person in the family.

D Dad is the .... person in the family.

E Brother is the .... person in the family.

F Grandma is the .... person in the family.

8 What about you? Ask and tell a friend.

Who is the oldest person in your family?

The oldest person in my family is Grandma.

Play Station 2

9 Read and match the questions and answers.

questions

A What's your name?

B Where do you live?

C What's your favourite sport?

D And are you good at skateboarding?

E What do you say to the other children?

answers

Yes! I'm the best skateboarder in town.

I live near the park.

Be safe! Always wear a helmet and protective pads.

Skateboarding, of course!

My name is Skater Boy.

6 **10 Listen and check.**

11 Listen. Say the poem. Then look, read, match and colour the frames.

I have a baby. He's my baby. He's mine.

You have a skateboard. It's your skateboard. It's yours.

She has a bag. It's her bag. It's hers.

He has a dream. It's his dream. It's his.

We have a game. It's our game. It's ours.

You have a mother. She's your mother. She's yours.

They have a friend. He's their friend. He's theirs.

Play Station Project

Skater Boy Game

Make and play your own board game.

You need:

1 piece of paper

1 piece of cardboard

ruler

pencil

colours

dice

4 different counters (buttons)

1 Either copy the picture on this page, or download and colour the game on our website.

2 Stick the game onto a piece of card.

3 Play the game with up to 4 friends. Put the counters on START. Before throwing the dice each player must spell a word from the story: "How do you spell 'hopscotch'?

4 If s/he spells the word correctly then s/he throws the dice and moves forward. If s/he lands on a skateboard square then s/he must follow the movement of the arrow.

5 The first player to arrive at FINISH, wins the game.

Go to www.helblingyoungreaders.com to download this page.